THE UNEXPURGATED ADVENTURES OF
SHERLOCK HOLMES

BOOK 5

THE ORANGES OF DEATH!

by NP Sercombe

The un-edited manuscript originally entitled
The Five Orange Pips written by
Dr. John Watson and Sir Arthur Conan Doyle

Illustrations by Emily Snape

Published by EVA BOOKS 2019 – c/o Harry King Films Limited
1&2 The Barn
West Stoke Road
Lavant
n/r Chichester
West Sussex PO18 9AA

A CIP catalogue record for this book is available from the British Library.

ISBN 978-1-9996961-4-6 (Hardback)

Book layout & Cover design by Clare Brayshaw.

Cover illustration by Emily Snape.

Set in Bruce Old Style.

Prepared and printed by: York Publishing Services Ltd
64 Hallfield Road, Layerthorpe, York YO31 7ZQ

Tel: 01904 431213

Website: www.yps-publishing.co.uk

THE UNEXPURGATED ADVENTURES OF

SHERLOCK HOLMES

Books in the Series:

Nicholas Sercombe is a writer and producer for film and television. He has been lucky enough to work in comedy for most of the Holocene period with some of the greatest performers and writers. He is most comfortable when reading Conan Doyle and even happier when re-writing these extraordinarily entertaining stories by Dr. John Watson.

Emily Snape is a coffee addicted, London based illustrator, who's work can be found internationally in books, magazines, on the web, television and even buses.

She studied at Central Saint Martins, Bristol and Kingston and is rarely found without a pencil in her hand. She loves sketching in the streets of London and thinks life is too short for matching socks.

For lovers of oranges who enjoy laughing

The Oranges of Death!

(published in The Strand in November 1891 as
THE FIVE ORANGE PIPS by Dr. John Watson
and Arthur Conan Doyle)

When I glance over my notes and records of the
Sherlock Holmes cases between the years '82 and
'90, I am faced by so many which present strange and
interesting features, that it is no easy matter to know
which to choose and which to leave. Some, however,
have already gained publicity through the newspapers,
and others have not offered a field for those peculiar
qualities which my friend possessed in so high a degree,
and which it is the object of these papers to illustrate.
Some, too, have baffled his analytical skill, and would
be, as narratives, beginnings without an ending, while
others have been but partially cleared up, and have
their explanations founded rather upon conjecture and
surmise than on that absolute logical proof which was
so dear to him. There is, however, one of these last
which give some account of it, in spite of the fact that
there are points in connection with it which never have
been, and probably never will be, entirely cleaned up.

The years of 1887 furnished us with a long series
of cases of greater or lesser interest, of which I retain
the records. Among my headings under this one of
twelve months, I find an account of the adventure of

the Paradol Chamber Pot, probably the dullest of our mysteries; of the Amateur Mendicant Society, which held a luxurious club in the lower vault of a well-marketed furniture warehouse; of the facts connected with the loss of the British barque-with-a-leak *Sophy Anderson*; of the dwarf-breeding culture of the Grice Patersons on the island of Uffa, and finally of the Camberwell Beauty poisoning case. In the latter, how, I ask you, could anyone have believed that a creature such as a venomous butterfly ever existed? Apart from this obvious lepidopteran flaw from the outset, Holmes was at his very best. He was able, by winding up the dead man's watch, to prove that it had been wound up two hours ago, and that therefore the deceased had gone to bed within that time – a deduction which was of the greatest importance in clearing up the case. All these I may sketch out at some future date, but none of them present such singular features as the strange train of circumstances which I have now taken up my pen to describe. Nothing, however, could have prepared us for the surprise that greeted us upon our return to Baker Street from Ross in Herefordshire, having just saved an innocent young man from the gallows.[*]

We arrived in London late in the evening, at about 8 o' clock, and the equinoctial gales had set in with exceptional violence. The wind was screaming and the rain beating down against us when Mrs. Hudson opened the front door. Holmes, who had been anxious enough on the railway journey to sit in stony silence throughout, his emerald eyes staring into infinity, his long white fingers fidgeting, now leaned forwards like a jockey about to start a race. Our landlady greeted us

---

[*]   see the account of *My First Proper Rural Murder*

in hushed tones. 'Mr. Holmes, I fear the end is most imminent for your Nanny. You could not have arrived a moment later. She is asking for you. Come this way, quickly now...'

Once the invitation had been made, he jumped forwards and followed up close behind Mrs. Hudson. I followed them. We weaved a path through the reception rooms of the ground floor, our landlady's living quarters. This was a new experience for Holmes and I; neither of us had ever been invited into her inner sanctum before. I did not have much time to reconnoitre because the journey through to the rear of the property was expedient and the mood was sombre, but I couldn't help but notice the delightful decoration, the rich Axminster, the exquisite possessions and Georgian furniture. Mrs. Hudson was a lady of exceptionally good taste, and clearly a woman of some means. This in itself was a revelation.

We arrived in a room that was a coal-hole, darkened to pitch black by the closed curtains, shutting out even the merest exterior night illumination. It was quiet too and very spooky. The space was lit by low level candles and there was a hint of incense in the air. There, in front of us, lay Elspeth Moriarty supine on the old oak bed, looking like she had been laid-out to die because my experienced eye told me that she had not passed over yet. Well, her chest was heaving. Otherwise, she was motionless and peaceful. I took a step closer to look at this much loved old trooper of Holmes's. Actually, upon viewing her exceptionally pale face, I realised she was not very old at all. Late fifties, maybe sixty? Hmm! I wondered what had brought this woman to death's front door. Her skin was a good colour, despite the waxiness of imminent death, and her flesh was fatty and plump, a far cry from the emaciation of a cancer. Maybe it was her heart that was failing her?

Holmes sat down on the counterpane by her side and took her hand in his. He leaned in close to her and said, 'Nanny, it is I, Sherlock.' Suddenly, her eyes flashed open – death's ghastly claw had not stolen this lady's spirit yet – and she lifted her right arm up. Her not-so-gnarled fingers pulled the top of his ear back. She peered inside it.

'You could grow potatoes in there,' said she, and her hand unfurled to deliver a smack to his cheek. 'Naughty boy!'

Holmes pulled back sharply. 'But Nanny, we were in Ross. There was no time for my evening bath. We travelled here as fast as we were able.'

'It just as well you did! I have something of the utmost importance to tell you.' She caught sight of me. 'Who is that Cheshire Cat with you?'

'May I introduce my companion, Dr. John Watson.' I leaned in closer to her and smiled even more effusively.

'What a grinning fellow he is!' she muttered. 'I don't need another doctor to tell me I am dying. Is it necessary for him to be here?'

Holmes patted her hand. 'Nanny, this is not Lewis Carroll. Anything you say to me, you must say with Watson beside me.' The troubled detective looked at me and indicated I should draw up a chair to sit beside him. This I did, eagerly. Nanny Moriarty looked at me again.

'Doctor, I am a funambulist on the cord of life itself, and I am about to reach the final pier. There, I shall fall off my perch for the last time. This time there will be no safety net to catch me. Please, help me along that cord, for just long enough to say what I must to Master Sherlock here.'

It was my duty to help her survive, not to let go, which was a tricky balance for a mere army doctor. I rummaged through my bag. Whatever I mixed together, she needed something to speed up her metabolism, not to relax her into submission. I started out with a phial of laudanum, in liquid form, and poured it into a mortar. I added lysergic acid, an amphetamine in powder, and gave it some extra wallop by tincturing with heroin. As I stirred up the concoction, Holmes patted Nanny's hand again and looked over at what I was doing. He leaned in close to me.

'You may as well add cocaine to that cocktail, Doctor.'

'So says the doctor of chemistry! And why?'

'Because you have got everything else in there, including the kitchen sink, we may as well take the opportunity to experiment on a live human being without any consequences.'

'Good idea, Holmes!' said I and went back to my bag to find a pamphlet of pure cocaine. Without the use of a table, it was quite a balancing act to accommodate the materials and the mortar on my lap. I fumbled badly as I opened up the sachet and dug my spoon into the powder.

'Here, let me help you,' said Holmes, and a set of familiar, long white fingers intercepted the loaded spoon. 'What's good for the goose ...' and he poured the cocaine into the mortar, 'is good for the gander,' and before I could stop him Holmes had revisited the sachet, excavated a second, generous spoonful and whisked it skilfully up his left nostril. He threw his head back and announced: 'It's been a long day!' which, I suppose, it had. Anyway, I watched on, helpless, and was about to rebuke him when Nanny became quite agitated.

'Have you two quite finished?' We both nodded. 'Good boys! Then, I shall begin. And you, Doctor, fill up that hypodermic. Quickly! Before it is too late.'

What followed, dear reader, was one of the most astonishing collection of revelations that I have ever heard in my life. The medicine that I administered kept her functioning for a while but an hour later Holmes placed Nanny's limp hand upon her lifeless torso and looked at me.

'There is no time to be mournful, Doctor,' he spoke, in a low, bass tone. 'We must swing into action. You have been made privy to the career of Europe's most revered criminal, Professor James Edward Moriarty. The Napoleon of crime. The spider in the centre of the web of wickedness. The hub in the wheel of villainy. The king of the criminal underworld. The sculpture in the middle of the maze of skullduggery. The Minotaur in the labyrinth of the crime underworld. The cockerel in the...'

Clang! That was the doorbell, which stopped Holmes in his tracks. We would not have to suffer any more of his metaphors! Strangely, Mrs. Hudson seemed not to hear the bell. Both of us stared at her a moment.

'Why, hark?' said I, glancing at her. 'Surely that is somebody at the door? Who could come tonight, at this very late hour? Some friend of yours, Mrs. Hudson?'

'None of my friends would be so rude as to call on me in the middle of the night. It will be street urchins.'

Sherlock Holmes insisted on testing my concoction before injecting Nanny Moriarty.

She stared at me for a moment, and then dropped her resolve. 'I suppose I shall have to go and shoo them away!' Mrs. Hudson left the room in a bustle.

'Maybe it is a client, then, Holmes?'

'If so, it is a serious case. Nothing less would bring a man out on such an evening of shricking weather and so late in the day. But I take it that it is more likely to be some crony of our landlady's and she is too embarrassed to tell us.'

'From what your Nanny has just told us, I hope that it isn't Professor Moriarty come here to claim his mother's corpse.'

'You are correct in your assumption, Doctor, that the Professor will be drawn to his mother's demise, but he would not dare step over the threshold whilst I am here. He knows that he would be a dead man.'

I was shocked! I had never heard my friend speak so strongly and never with so much *bravura*, even threatening to kill another human being.

'I remember every word that Nanny told us,' I said, 'but I had no idea that your relationship with this fellow had sunk to one of mortal combat.'

Before he could reply, Mrs. Hudson called out to us. We both made our way to the hallway. There we met a young man, some two-and-twenty at the outside, well-groomed and trimly clad with an air of refinement and delicacy in his bearing. The streaming umbrella which he held in his hand, and his long shining waterproof, told of the fierce weather through which he had come. He looked about himself furtively and, in the feint glare of the hallway lamp, I could see that his face was pale, and his eyes were heavy, like those of a man who is weighed down with some great anxiety. Once he had undressed from his raincoat, we ushered him up the stairs and into our apartment. Sherlock Holmes indicated a seat at one side of the fireplace and the young man sat himself down. Holmes sank into the chair opposite.

'I shall fetch the medicine!' I announced and made my way over to the sideboard drawing up alongside the whisky Tantalus. I poured three generous fingers of Uffa Malt, distinctive because it is distilled and produced entirely by dwarves, and it is very good value. This was just what the doctor ordered: firstly, to restore the young man's circulation; secondly, to revitalise our constitutions after our long journey from Ross and the prolonged death of Nanny Moriarty. I handed out the tumblers and perched on the settee.

'I owe you an apology,' our visitor said, raising his glass and sinking a mouthful of Uffa's cheapest. 'That is better, thank you. I trust that I am not intruding. I fear that I have brought some traces of the storm and the rain into your snug chamber.'

'You have travelled far. I see that you have come up from the south-west.'

'Yes, from Horsham.'

'That clay and chalk mixture which I see upon your toe-caps is quite distinctive.'

'I have come for advice.'

'That is easily got.'

'And help.'

'That is not always so easy.'

'I have heard of you, Mr. Holmes. I heard from Major Prendergast how you saved him in the Thomas The Tankerville Club Scandal.'

'Ah, of course. He was wrongfully accused of cheating at cards.'

'He said you could solve anything.'

'He said too much.'

'That you have never been beaten.'

'I have been beaten four times – three by men and once by a woman.'

'Stewards' enquiry!' I said. 'It is five, and two have been women.' Both men diverted their gazes towards me. 'May I remind you how Nanny said that she had given you a good hiding with the slipper *and* the cane?'

'Ha! It sounds like you were rather a naughty child, Mr. Holmes!' remarked our visitor, looking at the great detective and grinning to himself.

Holmes glared at me. He shoved his empty glass under my nose. 'Watson make best use of your serving skills,' said Holmes. I raised myself up and headed towards the Tantalus whilst I overheard Holmes dismissing my relevance to the minutiae of a new case with the usual "ignore him" and urged our visitor to start telling us his story.

'This is no ordinary case,' he said.

'None of those which come to me are,' said Holmes. 'I am the last court of appeal.'

'And yet I question, sir, whether, in all your experience, you have ever listened to a more mysterious and inexplicable chain of events than those which have happened in my own family.'

'You fill me with interest!' Holmes remarked, leaning towards the young man (and I'll swear I could see the top of each ear tilt forwards). 'Pray, give us the essential facts from the commencement, and I can afterwards question you as to those details which seem to me to be most important.'

'My name,' he said, 'is John Openshaw, but my own affairs have, so far as I can understand it, little to do with this awful business. It is a hereditary matter, so in order to give you an idea of the facts, I must go back to the commencement of the affair. Firstly, you must know that my grandfather had two sons – my uncle, Elias and my father, Joseph. My Father had a small factory at Coventry. He enlarged it at the time of the invention of bicycling. He was the patentee of the Openshaw unbreakable tyre and his business met with such success that he was able to sell it and retire upon a handsome competence.

My Uncle Elias emigrated to America, when he was a young man, and became a planter in Florida, where he was reported to have done very well. At the time of the war he fought in Jackson's army and afterwards under Hood, where he rose to be a colonel. When Lee laid down his arms my Uncle returned to his plantation, where he remained for three or four years. About 1869 or 1870 he came back to Europe, and took a small estate in Sussex, near Horsham. He had made a very considerable fortune in the States, and his reason for leaving them was his aversion to the negroes and his dislike of the Republican policy in extending the franchise to them. He was a singular man, fierce and quick-tempered, very foul mouthed when he was angry, and of a most retiring disposition. During all the years that he lived in Horsham I doubt if ever he set foot in the town. He had a garden and two or three fields around his house, and there he would take his exercise, though very often for weeks on end he would never leave his room. He drank a great deal of brandy, and smoked very heavily, but he would see no society, and did not want any friends, not even his own brother.'

I leaned over to fill Openshaw's glass. I glanced over to Holmes. We raised our eyes at each other in weary harmony. We had a mute understanding that, if we took on this case, we were likely to encounter an irascible, bawdy, drunk, racist, anti-social bigot. Or, as was usual in our cases, we were taking on yet another irascible, bawdy, drunk, racist, anti-social bigot!

'Would you look at what you are doing!' cried Openshaw, his tumbler filled nearly to the brim with the Uffa dwarf juice. I apologised, and he settled back down.

'Uncle Elias didn't mind me,' he continued. 'In fact, he took a fancy to me, for at the time when he saw me first, I was a youngster of twelve or so. That would be in the year 1878, after he had been eight or nine years in England. He begged my Father to let me live with him, and he was very kind to me in his way. When he was sober, he used to be fond of playing backgammon and draughts with me, and he would make me his representative both with the servants and with the tradespeople, so that by the time that I was sixteen I was quite the master of the house. I kept all the keys and could go where I liked and do what I liked, so long as I did not disturb him in his privacy. There was one singular exception, however, for he had a single room, a lumber-room up among the attics, which was invariably locked, and which he would never permit either me or anyone else to enter. With a boy's curiosity I have peeped through the keyhole, but I was never able to see more than a collection of old trunks and bundles, as would be expected in such a room.

One day – it was in March 1883 – a letter with a foreign stamp lay upon the table in front of the Colonel's plate. It was not a common thing for him to receive letters, for his bills were all paid in ready money, and he had no friends of any sort. "From India!" he said, as he took it up. "Pondicherry postmark! What can this be?" Opening it hurriedly, out there jumped five little dried orange pips, which pattered down upon his plate. I began to laugh at this, but the laugh was struck from my lips at the sight of his face. His lip had fallen, his eyes were protruding, his skin the colour of putty, and he glared at the envelope which he still held in his trembling hand. '"K.K.K."'he shrieked, and then: "My God, my God! My sins have overtaken me!"

'What is it Uncle?' I cried.

"Death" he said and rising from the table he retired to his room, leaving me palpitating with horror. I took up the envelope and saw scrawled in red ink upon the inner flap, just above the gum, the letter "K" three times repeated. There was nothing else save the five dried pips. What could be the reason of his overpowering terror? I left the breakfast table, and as I ascended the stairs, I met him coming down with an old rusty key, which must have belonged to the attic, in one hand, and a small brass box, like a cash box, in the other.

"They may do what they like, but I'll checkmate them still," said he, with an oath. "Tell Mary that I shall want a fire in my room today, and send for Fordham, the Horsham lawyer."

I did as he ordered, and when Mr. Fordham arrived, we stepped up to the room. The fire was burning brightly, and in the grate, there was a mass of black fluffy ashes, as of burned paper, while the brass box stood open and empty beside it. As I glanced at the box I noticed, with a start, that upon the lid were printed the "treble K" which I had read in the morning upon the envelope.

"I wish you, John," said my uncle, "to witness my Will. I leave my estate, with all its advantages and all its disadvantages to my Brother, your Father, whence it will, no doubt, descend to you. If you can enjoy it in peace, well and good! If you find you cannot, take my advice, my boy, and leave it to your deadliest enemy. I am sorry to give you such a two-edged thing, but I can't say what turn things are going to take. Kindly sign the paper where Mr. Fordham shows you."

I signed the paper as directed, and the lawyer took it away with him. The singular incident made, as you may think, the deepest impression upon me, and I pondered over it, and turned it every way in my mind without being able to make anything of it. Yet I could not shake off the vague feeling of dread which it left behind, though the sensation grew less keen as the weeks passed, and nothing happened to disturb the usual routine of our lives. I could see a change in my Uncle, however. He drank more than ever, and he was less inclined for any sort of society. Most of the time he would spend in his room, with the door locked upon the inside, but sometimes he would emerge in a sort of drunken frenzy and would burst out of the house and tear about the garden with a revolver in his hand, screaming out that he was afraid of no man, and that he was not to be cooped up, like a sheep in a pen, by man or devil. When these hot fits were over, however, he would rush tumultuously in at the door, and lock and bar it behind him, like a man who can brazen it out no longer against the terror which lies at the roots of his soul. At such time I have seen his face even on a cold day, glisten with moisture as though it were newly raised from a basin.

Well, to come to an end to the matter, Mr. Holmes, and not to abuse your patience and your stock of whisky, there came a night when he made one of those drunken sallies from which he never came back. We found him, when we went to search for him, face downwards in a little green-scummed pool, which lay at the foot of the garden. There was no sign of any violence, and the water was but two feet deep, so that the jury, having regard to his known eccentricity, brought in a verdict of suicide. But I, who knew how he winced from the very thought of death, had much ado to persuade myself that he had gone out of his way to meet it. The matter passed, however, and my Father entered into possession of the estate, and of some fourteen thousand pounds, which lay to his credit at the bank.'

'One moment,' Holmes interposed. 'Your statement is, I foresee, one of the most remarkable to which I have ever listened. Let me have the date of the reception by your Uncle of the letter, and the date of his supposed suicide.'

'The letter arrived on March the 10th 1883. His death was seven weeks later, upon the night of 2nd May.'

'Thank you, Mr. Openshaw,' said Holmes, who then proceeded to ask about the specifics of the letter – i.e. the posting office of origination, et cetera, et cetera. My eyes fixed upon our guest's empty tumbler and my mind soon wandered back to Nanny Moriarty's extraordinary revelations of earlier on. I thought about her life story, of how she had been brutally beaten by her husband just at the moment she gave birth to her son, the professor, and this was because the infant's eyes were of a different colour to his own. Then, how she had tried to stop him gambling away his fortune on rigged card games and fixed horse racing and being chained to the kitchen table, and beaten, for her protestations. Then, how she had found him carousing with young, soft-cheeked boys from Nellie Dean's and for three years prior refused to join her in the marital bed and had beaten her instead, a poor show for a man of the cloth. Eventually, how she had visited the mortuary to identify his corpse, nobody preparing her for the sight of the murderous dagger still protruding from his heart, breaking her own.

'WAITER!'

I looked up to see Holmes berating me, with a wry smile on his face. 'Watson! This is a thirsty lad. Please, whet his whistle.'

I filled the young man's tumbler and made a gratuitous topping up to my own and of Holmes's. Openshaw was excited, his nostrils flared and his eyes bright. He downed a generous mouthful, cleared his throat and then finished it off. This boy is fired up, I thought to myself, and he has a deep-seated problem. I filled him up again whilst setting my mind to work on him.

'When my Father took over the Horsham property, he, at my request, made a careful examination of the attic, which had always been locked up. We found the brass box there, although its contents had been destroyed. On the inside of the cover was a paper label, with the initials "K.K.K." repeated upon it, and

"Letters, memoranda, receipts and a register" written beneath. These, we presume, indicated the nature of the papers, which had been destroyed by Colonel Openshaw. For the rest, there was nothing of much importance in the attic, save a great many scattered papers and notebooks bearing upon my Uncle's life in America. Some of them were of the war time, and showed that he had done his duty well, and had borne the repute of being a brave soldier. Others were of a date during the reconstruction of the Southern States, and were mostly concerned with politics, for he had evidently taken a strong part in opposing the carpetbag politicians who had been sent down from the North.

Well it was the beginning of '84, when my Father came to live in Horsham, and all went well as possible with us until January of '85. On the fourth day after the New Year I heard my Father give a sharp cry of surprise as we sat together at the breakfast table. There he was, sitting with a newly-opened envelope in one hand and five dried orange pips in the outstretched palm of the other one. He had always laughed at what he called my cock-and-bull story about the Colonel, but he looked very puzzled and scared now that the same thing had come upon himself.

"Why, what on Earth does this mean, John?" he stammered.

My heart had turned to lead. 'It is a "K.K.K.,"' said I.

'He looked inside the envelope. "So it is," he cried. "Here are the very letters. But what is written above them?"

"Put the papers on the sundial," I read, peeping over his shoulder.

"What papers? What sundial?" he asked.

'The sundial we have in the garden. There is no other,' said I; 'but the papers must be those that are destroyed.'

"Bollocks!" said he, gripping hard at his courage. "We are in an Anglo-Saxon country here."

'Hence, the Anglo-Saxon language?' I added.

'Oh yes, Doctor!' said our visitor. 'Dad was a true Anglo-Saxon Englishman and spoke his Anglo-Saxon mind! He wasn't having any of this threat to his existence. He then asked me where the letter had come from. I looked at the postmark and told him it was from Dundee. "Some preposterous practical joke," said he. "What have I done to do with sundials and papers or Dundee? I shall take no notice of such nonsense!" I told him that I should certainly speak to the police. He said: "And be laughed at for my pains? Nothing of the sort!"

'Obviously...' I interjected, 'your father had encountered the Boys in Blue before!'

'Hear-hear, Doctor!' cried Holmes, and slapped his thigh. 'But please shut up.'

'Sorry, Holmes...' I replied. I looked over at the young man, who smiled and raised his empty tumbler. Once again, I grasped the decanter.

'So, I said to my Father: 'Then let me contact the police.'

"No, I forbid you!" he said. "I won't have a fuss made over such nonsense!"

'It was in vain to argue with him, for he was a very obstinate man, and I held back from my proposition. I went about, however, with a heart which was full of forebodings.

In the third day after the coming of the letter my Father went from home to visit an old friend of his, Major Freebody, who is in command of one of the forts upon Portsdown Hill. I was glad that he should go, for it seemed to me that he was farther from danger when he was away from home. In that, however, I was in error. Upon the second day of his absence I received a telegram from the Major, imploring me to come at once. My Father had fallen over one of the deep chalk-pits which abound in the neighbourhood and was lying senseless, with a shattered skull. I hurried to him, but he passed away without having ever recovered his consciousness. He had, as it appears, been returning from Fareham in the twilight, and as the country was unknown to him, and the chalk-pit unfenced, the jury had no hesitation in bringing a verdict of: "Death from accidental causes." Carefully as I examined every fact connected with his death, I was unable to find anything which could suggest the idea of murder. There were no signs of violence, no footmarks, no robbery, no record of strangers having been seen upon the roads. And yet I need not tell you that my mind was far from at ease, and that I was well-nigh certain that some foul plot had been woven around him.

In this sinister way I came into my inheritance. You will ask me why I did not dispose of it? I answer because I was well convinced that our troubles were in some way dependent upon an incident in my Uncle's life, and that the danger would be as pressing in one house as in another.

It was in January, '85, that my poor Father met his end, and two years and eight months have elapsed since then. I had begun to take comfort too soon, however;

yesterday morning the blow fell in the very shape in which it had come upon my Father.'

The young man took from his waistcoat a crumpled envelope, and, turning to the table, he shook out upon it five little dried orange pips.

'This is the envelope,' he continued. 'The postmark is London – eastern division. Within are the very words which were upon my father's last message. "K.K.K."; and then "Put the papers on the sundial."'

'What have you done?' asked Holmes.

'Nothing.'

'Nothing!'

Openshaw sank his face into his thin, boyish hands and started to sniff. Then, I am embarrassed to tell you, he cried. I felt sorry for the chap, even though his blubbing was a terribly feminine thing to do. I studied him for a moment and applied some of the great detective's methods. I could see that he didn't wear a wedding ring, so there was no wife looking after him. Then I noticed the unnecessary twitching movements of his hands and feet. I had seen this type of nervous insecurity in the past, usually with troopers that were stationed away from home for too long. This young man was overwrought, and for a reason that was as old as the hills. I shielded my mouth from the boy and whispered to Holmes:

'I say, Holmes, what this boy needs is a darned good woman.'

'Really? What are the symptoms?'

'He shakes. He trembles. His mind wanders. His eyes flick side to side, in a restless pursuit of mental peace. He is drinking quickly in large volumes with no apparent effect.'

'And so, what do you prescribe, Doctor?'

'The best medicine for him is an evening with a nice girl. We should send him off down to Mother Kelly's *post haste.*' I studied the man again, his head hanging, and his fingers wound around his face. I leaned forward and studied him close up. 'No, Holmes, this may be worse than I thought...' I sat back and pondered a moment. 'This boy does *not* need a nice girl, he needs the Billericay Beauties!'

'Doctor!' said Holmes, in a not-so hushed voice. 'This man is already in acute mortal danger! They would kill him before his pursuers got to him.'

'Not necessarily, Holmes. They have their compassionate sides.'

Mr. Openshaw may have been crying but he could hardly escape the essence of our conversation. He looked up at us.

'To tell the truth, gentlemen,' he said, 'I could not care less if they kill me! I live in fear of my life every moment of the day and night. I have felt helpless and now I feel helpless. I have felt like one of those poor rabbits when the snake is writhing towards it. I seem to be in the grasp of some restless, inexorable evil, which no foresight and no precautions can guard against. I live in sleepless fear. I am willing to take on any other risk to my life, or I shall despair!'

I tipped some more whisky into his glass. He rolled it around his tumbler and tipped it down his throat.

'Tut! Tut!' cried Sherlock Holmes. 'You must act, man, or you are lost! Nothing but energy can save you. This is no time for despair.'

*"Stop blubbing, man!" said I to our new client.
"What you need is a good woman"*

'I have acted, Mr. Holmes! I have been to see the police.'

I shot a glance at Holmes. His face was wrought with cynical alarm and then we both chuckled. This alarmed our young guest.

'What is up, gentlemen? I may be soaked with your afternoon tea here, but...' He tipped his empty tumbler up and used it like a spyglass to look at each one of us, 'I was told that the police force is supposed to uphold the law in this country?'

'Ah!' said Holmes, regaining his self-control. 'Yes, that is how the government sells their position in society. The reality is far removed. Anyway, what happened? What did they say?'

'They listened to my story with a smile. I am convinced that the inspector has formed an opinion that the letters are all practical jokes, and that the deaths of my relations were really accidents, as the jury stated, and were not to be connected with the warnings.'

'Ha! That is just what I expected!' cried Holmes, and then he gurned a contorted face at me. 'Dr. Watson and I know precisely who that is, Mr. Openshaw.' Holmes jumped up out of his chair and grabbed his soft cloth hat. He placed it upon his crown and inclined his head.

'INSPECTOR LESTRADE!' we chorused in unison.

'Well, no, actually it was not Lestrade. Apparently, he was out of town solving a murder case....'

We let it pass.

'I was interviewed by an Inspector Gregson,' said Openshaw. 'He said that he was a finer detective than Lestrade.'

'It makes no difference which one, Mr. Openshaw,' exclaimed Holmes, who then crouched down, his long legs creasing up like scissors, threw back his head, raised his clenched fist in the air, in a classic *Forsythe,* and shouted: 'THE MAN IS AN IMBECILE!' He waved his fist at the heavens. 'AN IMBECILE!' repeated he.

'Oh, it seems that I made a mistake!' wailed Openshaw. 'The one thing he did do, however, was to allow me a policeman for my protection.'

'Is that policeman with you tonight?'

'No, he is at home.'

Holmes went puce in the face with rage. 'THE FOOL!' he shouted, and this time, he shook both of his fists in the air. 'THE BLIND FOOL!' Then, he relaxed for a moment before looking at our client with some tenderness.

'You are vulnerable, Mr. Openshaw. Instead of consulting those buffoons you should have come to me sooner. Why did you not come at once?'

'I did not know about you, Mr. Holmes. Or you, Dr. Watson.'

Holmes and I exchanged glances. The boy was clearly a bumpkin who didn't read the newspapers or *The Strand* magazine.

'It was only today that I spoke to Major Prendergast about my trouble and was advised by him to come to you.'

'Now, let's see about our predicament here,' mused Holmes. 'We should have acted before this. You have had this letter already two days? You have no further evidence, I suppose, than that which you have placed before us – no suggestive detail which might help us?'

'There is one thing,' said John Openshaw. He rummaged in his coat pocket clumsily – the whisky was having its effect – but eventually he drew out a piece of discoloured, blue-tinted paper. He laid it out upon the table. 'I have some remembrance,' said he, 'that on the day when my uncle burned the papers, I observed that the small, unburned margins which lay amid the ashes were of this particular colour. I found this single sheet upon the floor of his room, and I am inclined to think that it may be one of the papers which had, perhaps, fluttered out from among the others, and in that way may have escaped destruction. Beyond the mention of pips, I do not see that it helps us much. I think myself that it is a page from some private diary. The writing is undoubtedly my Uncle's.'

Holmes moved the lamp, and we both bent over the sheet of paper, which showed by its ragged edge that it had indeed been torn from a book. It was headed: "March 1869," and beneath were the following enigmatical notices:

'4th – Hudson came. Same old platform.

'7th – Set up the pips on McCauley, Paramore, and Swain of St. Augustine.

'9th – McCauley cleared.

'10th – John Swain cleared.

'12th – Visited Paramore. All well.

'Thank you,' said Holmes, folding up the paper and returning it to our visitor. 'And now you must on no account lose another instant. We cannot spare time even to discuss what you have told me. You must get home instantly, and act.'

Mr. Openshaw rose from his seat. He was unsteady on his feet. 'What shall I do?' he enquired of the great detective.

'There is but one thing to do. It must be done at once. You must put this piece of paper which you have shown us into the brass box which you have described. You must also put in a note to say that all the other papers were burned by your uncle, and that this is the only one which remains. You must assert that in such words as will carry conviction with them. Having done this, you must at once put the box out upon the sundial, as directed. Do you understand?'

'Yes. Entirely.'

'Do not think of revenge, or anything of the sort, at present. I think that we may gain that by means of the law; but we have our web to weave, while theirs is already woven. The first consideration is to remove the pressing danger which threatens you. The second is to clear up the mystery, and to punish the guilty parties.'

'I thank you,' said the young man, pulling on his overcoat with some whisky clumsiness. 'You have given me fresh hope. I shall certainly do as you advise.'

'Do not lose an instant. And, above all, take great care of yourself in the meanwhile, for I do not think there can be a doubt that you are threatened by a very real and imminent danger. How do you go back to Horsham?'

'By train from Waterloo.'

'It is nine-thirty. The streets will be lowly-populated. I must insist that you take a hansom to the railway station. I trust you may travel in safety. And yet you cannot guard yourself too closely.'

'I am armed.' Mr. Openshaw pulled out a small revolver from his coat pocket.

'That may serve you well,' said Holmes. 'What do you say Doctor?'

'Indeed, and do not hesitate to use it, Mr. Openshaw. There is no better alternative than to shoot your enemy. Talking of which...'

Seeing Openshaw's small handgun reminded me of my own, new possession. It was an impressive weapon acquired by my nephew, William, the practice manager of my consulting rooms in South Kensington whom I had sent on a mission for an old army revolver and he returned with something much grander. I hadn't even shown it to my friend yet, so I rushed over to the Chippendale escritoire.

'My young William has found me a revolver with a difference.' I remarked on my way.

'You do not need to remind me,' said Holmes tetchily, 'Mr. Openshaw is... well, perhaps you could show me later... Oh, Watson! THAT is a BEAST!'

I presented the gleaming Holland revolver to Holmes.

'My boy William did me proud, Holmes. He picked it up for a mere half a crown.'

He took the gun from my hand, his eyes wide open in wonder. Openshaw's jaw hung down in an ungainly manner.

'That is twice the size of my own!' he said in wonder. 'What IS IT?'

'This,' said Holmes, marvelling at its hexagonal barrel, then flicking it around expertly in his hand until his fingers clasped the walnut grip, '...is a point five-seven-seven Henry Holland five-shooter. Holland named it "The Boxer" because its bullets deliver a knock-out punch.'

Holmes paused, only for dramatic effect I am sure, and then looked at us gravely.

'However,' he whispered, 'the consequence of such a heavy ordnance is a recoil so violent that the user must hold the gun just so, with both hands...' Holmes gripped my revolver firmly. He spread his long legs into a braced stance and dropped his long arms to their full extent, the gun pointing now at the floor, '...and keep moving whilst it is in operation.' Holmes swung his arms upwards in a flowing movement. Halfway through this arc he pretended to pull the trigger and shoot at an imaginary object in the distance.

'Bang! A man may break his wrist if he does not maintain the movement.'

'Well, Holmes, I have to say that I had no idea I had purchased a small cannon!'

'This revolver became known as the "Manstopper" and rightly so because anybody misfortunate enough to be caught on the receiving end of this weapon is maimed so badly, he is surely killed. It soon became obsolete.' He handed the gun back to me. 'The perfect side arm for a funeral director.'

'Not for a doctor?' I enquired.

'For a doctor who likes to write death certificates.'

Oh! Sheepishly, I placed the "Manstopper" softly upon the occasional table adjacent. I stood back to admire the potential of its powerful capability. Trouble was, now I was in great trepidation of using it! No one would want a weapon like this. Suddenly, it dawned on me why the gun was only half a crown!

'I think I shall stick to my own gun, thank you' said Openshaw pocketing his small weapon. 'And I shall make my journey home in better spirits!' he exclaimed. Then, instead of heading towards the door, he wobbled over to me. He lowered his voice.

'I say, Doctor, could you give me some directions to that establishment you mentioned earlier? The one with the Billericay Beauties?'

'Mother Kelly's? Why, it is in Kingly Street, just off Regent Street. Tell Madame...'

'NO!' cried Holmes. 'No, Mr. Openshaw! You have had this letter already two days. Your life is in peril! GO STRAIGHT TO WATERLOO STATION! I shall set to work on your case tomorrow.'

'I shall see you at Horsham, then?'

'No, your secret lies here in London. It is here that I shall seek it.'

'Then I shall call upon you in a day, or in two days, with news as to the box and the papers. I shall take your advice in every particular.' He shook hands with us and took his leave, wavering unsteadily as he walked out of the door. Holmes and I followed him out and watched him intently as he lurched and stumbled unevenly down the stairs, each of us bearing an anguished expression until he reached the hallway without falling down. Once he was through the door, Holmes looked at me.

'Watson. The man walks like a parrot.'

'In army vernacular, he is as pissed as a parrot, but I have to say, Holmes, that I am concerned for the young man's safety.' I turned to look at my friend and opened my arms in entreaty. 'Surely we should accompany him to the railway station?'

Holmes weighed up the argument. 'Watson, you are right. Fetch your army revolver and let us make haste!' We dived back into the apartment. He marched over to the cloak stand and grabbed his portmanteau. I rushed over to the (reproduction) Chippendale Escritoire and grabbed the gun and my mackintosh. We ran down the staircase after him.

* * *

Outside on Baker Street the wind screamed and the rain splashed against the pavement. We had just enough time to shout out loud at Mr. Openshaw before he ascended into a four-wheeler, but he gave us no acknowledgement. We could not be heard because of the wild elements, blown in upon us like a sheet of seaweed in a gale, and now absorbing our voices. We threw our dignity aside and ran after the cab as it set off, but we were too late and could not catch it. By good fortune, there was another four-wheeler within hailing distance. We climbed in and gave the driver instructions to not lose sight of it, whatever happened on the road and whatever it took. I told him that a man's life was at stake and that there was a golden guinea in it for his sympathetic reaction. At the sight of the shiny coin the man's eyes lit up. We shot off in zealous pursuit down Baker Street, with no sparing of the horses.

Naturally, one would have expected Mr. Openshaw's four-wheeler to be travelling at a moderate pace towards Waterloo Station but when I leaned out of the window of our cab I was surprised by the high speed of our client's vehicle. I calculated we were not making up any ground. But then I saw the young man's head peer out of his own window, stare back at us for a moment and then urge his driver on. But then it dawned on me... My goodness! He thought that we were his potential murderers! His driver lashed his whip up high in the air and I could hear him ya-ya-yahing all the way through Portman Square. We gave chase. We were travelling at such a high speed that I'll swear I saw the inside wheels lift off the road as his carriage turned left onto Oxford Street. We had embarked upon a self-perpetuating spiral of competitiveness – in other words, we were in a race!

I heaved myself back inside the carriage and planted myself on the driver's-side bench, where I clenched my buttocks tight and gripped the underside of the seat. Opposite me, the great detective was being thrown around the rear couch like a hot chestnut on a pikey's brazier.

'I say, Holmes, there is something up with young Openshaw.'

'Dammit! There's "something up" with the suspension on this carriage!'

'He thinks that we are the "K.K.K." chasing him through London!'

'Dear God! This was your idea, Watson...'

As we followed left onto Oxford Street, the carriage lurched violently to the right. I lost my grip and was shot across the compartment like a ball from a cannon, straight into Sherlock Holmes's lap. He became very agitated! Using immense upper body strength, he lifted me up from his lap, turned me over like a playing card and dropped me onto the floor.

'For goodness sakes, Watson, do try and control yourself!'

I looked up at him in astonishment. 'Holmes! I am fourteen stones and you tossed me around like a child's doll. How on Earth did you manage that?'

'It is my personal martial art, tailor-made by Kanō Jigorō, the Japanese prodigy: a Russian Sambo that is a portmanteau for samozaschcita bez oruzhiya, with a Pankration influence.'

I shouldn't have asked... but I did, didn't I?

'Very impressive, Holmes! Good old Kanō Jigorō!'

'Good old Jigorō was eleven years old when I entered his tutelage.'

Admonished and embarrassed, I crawled back onto my seat. 'I fear for our client, Holmes. Why would he need to travel at such high speed when his only requirement is to catch a train to Horsham?'

'I agree, Watson. It is highly suspicious. I suggest we hold tight and let our driver make his best efforts. He seems to know what he is doing.'

'It's a fine strategy, Holmes, but it is mighty uncomfortable!'

We hurtled down Oxford Street, a filthy boulevard patronised by greasy foreigners and lined with sixpenny shops selling cheap, tawdry goods, a road so awful I named it the "bum crack of London." Naughty, I know, but it was a fact. The bum crack was a straight line, which meant a rapid passage down it and allowed me the chance to lean back out of the window. We were making ground. I could see Openshaw's four-wheeler more clearly but I noticed that Oxford Circus was coming up and so I dropped back down inside the compartment and shouted a warning of: 'Hold on tight!' to my companion.

'Regent Street?' he enquired, as he clamped his fingers around the edge of his nearest coachwork.

I just had time to nod and latch onto my seat before the carriage lurched violently to the right. We were hurled to the left side of the compartment. This time, however, both of us held on to our positions. We straightened back up and relaxed. I smiled and rubbed my hands together in glee.

'My, what fun! The road is straight now for a while...'

Suddenly, the carriage swerved to the left, turning into Great Marlborough Street instead of heading down Regent Street. Holmes and I were catapulted into the righthand side of the compartment, my perfect gnashers planting into the leather upholstery; Holmes's large head flattening his top hat to a dinner plate. Both of us finished up in crumpled heaps, legs akimbo between the seats and the floor. Holmes cried out something indistinguishable; I let out a muffled curse. Goodness it was painful! What was Openshaw doing? Again, we lurched as the carriage took another turn, this time to the right but fortunately at a lower speed. Where was he headed to?

'Kingly Street!' uttered the great detective. 'Openshaw is heading for you-know-where.'

'For you-know-what,' I added.

'Yes! And this is all your doing, Watson! It was YOU who filled him to the brim with the Uffa dwarf juice. It was YOU who implanted the idea of a visit to Mother Kelly's. Otherwise we would be on our way to Waterloo Station, and my hat would be as good as new.'

'Yes, Holmes. Sorry, Holmes.'

I leaned out of the window. Our driver continued to urge our cab down the narrow street, horses at the gallop, even though Mr. Openshaw's was pulling up outside the famous knocking-shop. Innocent pedestrians were forced out of the way, some of them shouting and cursing. I watched in dismay as we drew up alongside the Openshaw four-wheeler, noisily, and then swerved across its way forwards, with a screeching of metal against cobble and reigned up in an emergency-stop of snorting beasts. Suddenly, I was parallel with the window of Openshaw's carriage. Unfortunately, due to Holmes's incessant warnings about his life being in great danger, Mr. Openshaw assumed me to be his prospective murderer. He drew his revolver and fired several shots! Luckily, he was hopeless. Three bullets ricocheted off local buildings and one embedded itself in the side of the carriage. This caused chaos! Men were shouting. Women were crying. Horses were screaming. I dropped back inside the carriage and onto the floor where I found the great detective lying prone. He grabbed me, affectionately, by the shirt collar.

'For Christ's sakes, Watson, shoot him!'

'I cannot shoot a client, Holmes!' Then I looked at the "Manstopper" in my hand, large and magnificent and gleaming imminent destruction. 'Especially with this...' But then I wondered what it would be like to fire a shot. Seeing as the great detective had asked me to extricate us from this awkward situation, I crawled back up the door, popped my head above the panel and pulled the hammer back on the point five-seven-seven "Manstopper." I shouted out loud: 'Mr. Openshaw! It is I, Dr. Watson and Mr. Sherlock Holmes!'

I aimed the revolver straight up into the night sky. I closed my eyes. I squeezed the trigger and suddenly it went off: BOOM! The bomb that exploded in my hands was like nothing I had ever experienced before! It was so violent that it blew me off my feet. I was hurled back into the carriage compartment, skittling Sherlock Holmes just rising from the floor. We fell into a heap, one on top of the other.

After a few moments of blinding shock, we started to pick ourselves up. The great detective was underneath me, holding his ears and moaning in pain. I was first up on my knees. My ears were ringing a muffled whining sound. My head was throbbing like a giant heart! Plomp! Plomp! Plomp! I looked down at the great detective and he was shouting at me, but I could not hear what he said, so I pulled myself up and peered over the door panel. My goodness, the whole street had emptied! I looked over to Openshaw's carriage. He popped his head out of the window, looked at me and, so I was told later, he cried out: 'My God, it's you! You and your new toy, Doctor. I thought that you were the "K.K.K.!"'

And before I could say anything to him, he jumped out of his carriage and scurried into the knocking-shop.

* * *

We had taken one of the upstairs rooms in the rabbit warren of a building that was Mother Kelly's. Openshaw had ensconced himself with the Billericay Beauties in a room directly above us and, as one would expect in a *ménage à trois*, they were making one hell of a racket! Our room was one of the smaller, private,

*Shooting our clients was a completely new feature
in our adventures!*

sitting rooms; no bedroom furniture for extraneous activities, just comfortable sofas and chairs. The walls were decorated in brothel-burgundy damask, the curtains a heavy bottle-green velvet and the furniture adorned with brocade in abundance. But what made Mother Kelly's *the* stand-out knocking-shop of London Town was undoubtedly the hand-picked harlots, all taught meticulously in the fine arts of seduction by Madame herself. By combining the two, she had created a tasteful ambience of the most excellent quality. The customers could enjoy her graduates on the most elegant furniture and admire the finest porcelain and statues that adorned the pilasters and tables at the same time, usually in the throes of ecstasy. This den of iniquity housed one of the most stylish collections of erotic art outside the Vatican; Greek gods fornicating with one other, some conjugating with compliant mortals and others subjugating wild animals with their lustful deviations. Mother Kelly was a clever woman; she was an art collector, a seductress and a sublime hostess, which meant that members of Society rubbed shoulders with the nabobs and the wealthiest of foreigners in this exceptional establishment. We were fortunate enough to be highly valued clientele within this clique.

Sherlock Holmes sat for some time in silence, in the red glow of the fire, with his head sunk forward and his eyes bent down upon his lap. Then he lit his pipe. Leaning back in his chair he watched the blue smoke-rings as they chased each other up to the ceiling.

'I think, Watson,' he remarked at last, 'that of all our cases, we have had none more fantastic than this.'

'Save, perhaps, the Sign of Four.'

'Well, yes. Save, perhaps, that. And yet this John Openshaw seems to me to be walking amid even greater perils than the Sholtos.'

'Really, Holmes, you think that?'

'Yes, I do.'

'You really, really think that, do you?'

'Shut up, Watson. I am struggling to think clearly on this case.'

And that deficiency was hardly surprising, considering that the gorgeous Chantelle, a French courtesan of exceptional beauty, was below stairs maintaining the great detective's plumbing. This beautiful girl practiced with stylish technique, borne, I presume, from a great affection for her craft. I made a mental note to book in advance of my next visit. I watched her perform for a second or two, just to remind me – my goodness, I was reminded! – and then looked away again but I continued to tease Holmes for not giving her his full attention.

'Are you struggling, Holmes? Really, really struggling?'

'Yes! IF I could get up, Watson, I'd give you a p..p.. punch on the n..n..nose!'

'Ha! IF you could. But you cannot. Ha, ha! So, tell me, Holmes, have you formed any definite opinion as to what Openshaw's perils are?'

'There can be no question as to their nature,' he whispered stressfully, 'but please, Watson, old friend, I am trying to c..c...concentrate!'

'Now come along, Holmes. I know that you cannot resist telling me.'

'R..r...RIGHT NOW,' he seethed through gritted teeth, 'he will be trying to survive the lethal duet of the B..B..Billericay Beauties, working him over like the s..st...starving harpies of Tartarus. You know all about them.'

My eyes glazed over a moment whilst memories flashed through my mind. 'Indeed, I do, Holmes, and never again. I was in hospital for two days afterwards.' I looked over at him and, to my delight, he was in a hell of a battle; his enormous brain fighting to deliver the detailed analysis of his detective work to me whilst being overpowered by the sensations that Chantelle was introducing to his body. I smiled to myself – revenge was sweet!

'It was actually th...th...three days...D..D... Doctor!' He pointed to the room upstairs. 'So, maybe they will k...k... kill him before this "K.K.K" .... can get their hands on him.

'Ah, what a devilish *ménage* he must be in! But, Holmes, who is this "K.K.K." and why does he pursue this unhappy family?'

This time there was no reply. I looked over. There was no doubt that Chantelle, the valiant warrioress, was winning. Sherlock Holmes had prostrated himself, his head hard back in his chair, his eyes closed and his body rigid, undoubtedly as a precursor to the inevitable. I was too embarrassed to watch him in his moment of ecstasy. I shifted my position on the sofa, turning away. I studied my fingernails for a second or two but was then distracted by horrendous noises from the room above: furious snorting, two spooky wails smattered with intermittent screams and a rendering of what sounded like wood and metal. Would Openshaw survive the encounter and ever make it to Waterloo railway station? Maybe not... Fortunately, then, I spied a copy of *The Strand* magazine on the table adjacent. I grabbed it and ripped it open, bringing the pages up close to my face. I flicked through the pages, rustling them as much as I could to block out any anticipated gasps of exultation, but there were none. The room had become very quiet. Behind us, I heard the door open and close. I dropped the magazine and swung round to my original position. Well I never! He was sitting there fully-dressed with his elbows placed upon the arms of his chair, his fingertips steepled together, the master detective in deep pontification, and looking as calm and collected as a country pastor reviewing his stamp collection! There was a slight flush to his cheeks but otherwise there was absolutely no evidence of the recent pip-pip from Chantelle. It was as if the clock had been wound back, as if the last ten minutes had never happened. As I have informed you in the past, dear reader, Sherlock Holmes devoted only brief moments of his life to satiate his base physiological needs. Then, it was back to business as usual.

'Ah, there you are Doctor...' he continued. 'As I was saying, the ideal reasoner would, when he had once been shown a single fact in all its bearings, deduce from it not only all the chain of events which led up to it, but also all the results which would follow from it. As Cuvier would correctly describe a whole animal by the contemplation of a single bone, so the observer who has thoroughly understood one link in a series of incidents should be able to accurately state all the other ones, both before and after. We have not yet grasped the results which the reason alone can attain to. Problems may be solved in the study which have baffled all those who have sought a solution by the aid of their senses. To carry the art, however, to its highest pitch, it is necessary that the reasoner should be able to utilise all the facts which have come to his knowledge; and this in itself implies, as you will readily see, a possession of all knowledge, which, even in these days of free education and encyclopedias, is a somewhat rare accomplishment. It is not so impossible, however, that a man should possess all knowledge which is likely to be useful to him in his work, and this I have endeavoured in my case to do. If I remember rightly, you on one occasion, in the early days of our friendship, defined my limits in a precise fashion by assessing my abilities and scoring my strengths and weaknesses on a scale of one to ten.'

'Yes,' I answered, chuckling. 'It was a singular document, more of a score chart. For instance, you scored zero points on philosophy, astronomy, and politics. Geography was only a two. Botany was a surprising seven to nine points.'

'May I remind you, sir, that botany is my mother's doctorate – I grew up in a home that was crammed full of the indigenous flora of this country.'

'Indeed, and it has rubbed off on you, but you are hardly perfect. However, I scored you ten out of ten for geology, when studying the mud stains from any region within fifty miles of Town. Chemistry: sublimely brilliant and ten points, but eccentric and wild. Anatomy: an unsystematic five. A sensational ten points for literature, and for crime records a unique eleven. Also, above seven points for each of being a violin player, boxer, swordsman, lawyer, and self-poisoner by cocaine and tobacco. Those, I think, were the main points and scoring of my analysis.'

Holmes grinned at the last item. 'Your *anal* analysis...' he said, and then laughed. 'I say now, as I said then, that a man should keep his little brain-attic stocked with all the furniture that he is likely to use, and the rest he can put away in the lumber-room of his library, where he can get it if he wants it.'

'You did, Holmes, you did. Do you remember that I also recounted a different point-scoring definition from my days in the army? It graded and marked one's prowess with the fairer sex and was an amusing weekly calculator in the mess. We called it "Lads' Points."'

'Yes, I do. Where points are awarded for female conquests, the maximums scoring the highest for the most extraordinary and the most depraved, preferably a mixture of the two?'

'Yes, Holmes.'

'It was amusing, but silly, Watson.' All of a sudden, a hammering sound seeped through the ceiling from the room above, accompanied by one of the girls shrieking in falsetto. 'Right now, we should discard that silliness and concentrate on the case we have in hand.'

'Boooo!'

'Watson! May I remind you that our client is situated only a few feet above our heads when he should be on the fast train to Horsham.' He snatched his hunter to find out the time. 'A few minutes more – that is all – and then we go up there and drag him out. Do you agree?'

From above, a saw could be heard rasping against metal form. 'Hark, Holmes! Listen to that! There can be no doubt that he is still up there enjoying himself.'

*Openshaw's blood-curdling screams from above
made us lose our appetites.*

'That, Watson, I do not doubt. He is safe at the moment, but the only way that he can absolve himself from his relative's dreadful legacy, and for him to survive, is by reaching his house tonight where he must carry out my instructions to the letter. Surely he must finish off soon?' He looked up at the ceiling. His fingers drummed the sofa cushions. 'In the meantime, we need to muster all our resources to solve this mystery. I have brought with me one volume of the *American Encyclopedia*.'

'Of course, you have!' I sneered sarcastically. This was a ridiculous claim! I was absolutely, one hundred per cent certain, that he had not had the time to pick up a socking great book before we raced out of the door just now. 'My dear Holmes, you must take me for a complete fool. When we left Baker Street, we were in considerable haste. Quite simply, there was no time available.' I laughed out loud and slapped my thigh. 'And then you managed to make it completely invisible during our haywire journey over here. Hmmm? I think not.'

He was nonplussed. 'Is that so, my unobservant friend?' Holmes leered back. He rummaged around in his portmanteau and picked out a volume of the *American Encyclopedia* marked "K". I recognised it, dammit! He must have grabbed it whilst I was finding my revolver. He turned his head slowly, to engage my attention, and curled his upper lip at me whilst opening it up. 'Now,' he said, 'if you are sitting less cynically, let us consider the situation and see what may be deduced from it. In the first place, we may start with a strong presumption that Colonel Openshaw had some very strong reason for leaving America. Men

-44-

at his time of life do not change all their habits and exchange willingly the charming climate of Florida for the lonely life of an English provincial town. His extreme love of solitude in England suggests the idea that he was in fear of someone or something, so we may assume a working hypothesis that it was fear of someone or something which drove him from America.'

Holmes was in one of those moods where he becomes the teacher and I the pupil, but I was tired and feeling sleepy so I let him do it. I started to nod off but suddenly I heard a thump and a groan from up above us and felt a twinge of randiness! I sprung out of my seat with a 'carry on, Holmes, carry on...'

'As to what it was that he feared,' he continued, as I opened the door and collared one of the knocking-shop staff, 'we can only deduce that by considering the formidable letters which were received by himself and his successors. Did you make note of the postmarks of those letters?'

I sat back down in my chair. 'I did. The first was from Pondicherry,' I resummarised for him, 'the second from Dundee, and the third from London.'

'From East London. What do you deduce from that?'

'That they are all seaports. That the writer was on board a ship.'

'Excellent, Watson!'

There was a gentle knock on the door. I looked over at my companion. 'What do you deduce from that?'

'That you have requested the attention of Subaha, known in here as the "Delhi Home Delivery" to both fulfil your latent envy of my encounter with Chantelle, your burgeoning libido from overhearing Openshaw's activities and, finally, to prevent you falling asleep.'

'Holy of the Holies, Holmes!' I ejaculated. 'How did you know that?'

'It is elementary, Watson. I shall continue...'

I heard the door open and click shut. Sure enough, in walked the most beautiful of all of Mother Kelly's eastern girls, the exquisite Subaha. Holmes held back from continuing his sermon momentarily and started to twiddle his long white fingers impatiently, seemingly playing an invisible pianoforte, but secretly envious. Subaha drew up a little footstool and placed it in front of me. She settled herself down into a comfortable position. Holmes rolled his eyes heavenward, put his hand up to his better side and looked away. He, also, could not watch his best friend playing snooker with a professional! Meanwhile, Subaha had got hold of me and made a start.

'Now may I please continue, Doctor?' he said, addressing the bookshelves on the far wall.

'P...p...please! Holmes, you m..m...mustn't stop on my account...'

'I wasn't. Now, we have already a clue. There can be no doubt that the probability – the strong probability – is that the writer of the letters was on board a ship. And now let us consider another point. In the case of Pondicherry seven weeks elapsed between the threat and its fulfilment; in Dundee it was only some three or four days. Does that suggest anything?'

'A g..g..GREATER distance to t..t..travel?'

'But the letter had also a greater distance to come.'

'NGNNGGNN!'

'There is at least a presumption that the vessel in which the man or men are is a sailing ship.'

'Goodness Holmes, a sh...sh..ship of the se..se... *sailing* variety?'

'Shut up Watson! Just listen! It seems to me that they always sent their singular warning or token before them when starting upon their mission. You see how quickly the deed followed the sign when it came from Dundee. If they had come from Pondicherry in a steamer they would have arrived almost as soon as their letter. But as a matter of fact, seven weeks elapsed. I think that those seven weeks represented the difference between the mail boat which brought the letter, and the sailing... *vessel* which brought the writer.'

'Yes! Keep going, dear...Holmes...whatever.... Yes!'

'Yes, it is probable. And now you see the deadly urgency of this new case, and why I urged young Openshaw to caution. The blow has always fallen at the end of the time which it would take the senders to travel the distance. But this one comes from London, and therefore we cannot count upon any delay.'

'G...G...Good God, Holmes! If you say so!' I cried.

'Are you still in *ante-extremis*, Doctor?' Remember, dear reader, that Holmes had his face turned away from me.

'I... I... She has only just s..st...started!' I saw him nod his head.

'Then I shall continue relaying the facts. The papers which Openshaw carried are obviously of vital importance to the person or persons in the sail... in the ship. I think that it is quite clear that there must be more than one of them. A single man could not have carried out two deaths in such a way as to deceive a coroner's jury. There must have been several in it, and they must have been men of resource and determination. Their papers they mean to have, be the holder of them whom it may. In this way you see "K.K.K."ceases to be the initials of an individual and becomes the badge of a society.'

All of a sudden, he spun around to face me, his face beaming. Then, to my surprise, he jumped up from his chair, rushed over to where I was, and dropped himself down onto the sofa next to me. He was in a state of excitement, his features all determined and animated, and now only inches from my own. Subaha, bless her, didn't even break stride, but she was looking up now at us both with wonder in her eyes.

'Have you never heard of the Ku Klux Klan?!' he cried, looking straight at me, the forefinger of his right hand jabbing the air exultantly. 'Here it is!' he continued, presenting me with the *Encyclopedia* book wide open on my chest. 'Here, let me read it to you.' He wrenched the book away and laid it on his lap in front of him. "The word Ku Klux Klan. A name derived from a fanciful resemblance to the sound produced by cocking a rifle. This terrible secret society was formed by some ex-Confederate soldiers in the Southern States after the Civil War, and it rapidly formed local branches in different parts of the country, notably in Tennessee. Louisiana, the Carolinas, and Florida. Its power was used for political purposes, principally for terrorising the negro voters, and the murdering or driving from the country of those who were opposed to its views. Its outrages were usually preceded by a warning sent to the marked man in some fantastic but generally recognised shape – a sprig of oak leaves in some parts, melon seeds or" listen to this, Watson –"*orange pips* in others!"'

'F..fe-fe...fe-fe...fa...fascinating!'

Holmes was triumphant, his forefinger pricking the air towards the ceiling and the room up above. The *ménage à trois* upstairs must have been jolted by the great detective's energetic gesture because just at that moment there was a massive CRASH! and a blood-curdling scream, the style of which I had only heard when I was an army surgeon in the field hospitals of Afghanistan. It was the type that was always followed by silence, and this one was typical.

'Hello?' Holmes pondered. 'Even by their standards, that sounds extreme...'

'THAT is not a cry of ecstasy...THAT is a scream of DEATH!'

Holmes's eyes widened.

'For Pete's sake, I am a Doctor!'

He leapt up onto his feet and made a dash for the door. Subaha disconnected and scurried away on all fours towards the curtains. I was left on my posterior, and in a state of extreme discomfort.

'Quickly, Watson!' He wrenched the door open. 'Come along! Make sure your revolver is loaded.' He ran out of the room at top speed towards the staircase.

From where I was sitting, I had no choice but to make a move. I looked over to Subaha, who was quivering most cheekily behind the green velvet, and decided she would be safest where she was. I stood up and fastened buttons to respectability, then I marched to the door, checking the weapon in my pocket, knowing that it was still fully loaded. Dammit!

* * *

Holmes and I ran through the door of the room above and stopped still in our tracks, agog. Some would call it a bedroom, but the sight that greeted us made me think that we had arrived in Mr. Allen's butcher shop. There, in front of us, was the disturbing sight of John Openshaw perching on a three feet high bench, positioned on his front, his arms and legs folded together, tucked in tight and trussed-up within a bizarre wire frame. He was the epitome of grotesqueness, his body glistening with oil and an apple sticking out of his mouth; his face locked in a spine-chilling grin. The Billericay Beauties were lying on the floor nearby, unconscious.

I rushed over to Openshaw. Holmes shut the door and locked it – he wished to prevent Mother Kelly's bully boys running in and despoiling evidence – before marching over to the open window where the wind and rain crashed through and howled around the room. Whilst he inspected every edge and contour for traces of human activity, he shouted after me to divert my attention to the girls. I stopped to look at them *en route*; they were, thank God, very much alive and starting to make a recovery from their faint.

I examined the gruesome remains of John Openshaw. His eyelids were retracted back into his skull, as far back as they were able, which exaggerated the protrusion of his eyeballs. He was staring into oblivion, with eyes like marbles. I had never seen anyone look like it before. Was this a man who had been frightened to death? On closer inspection, the reason for his demise became more obvious, so the answer was No, certainly not! There was a metal hawser knotted tight around his throat which was attached to a truss. The truss itself was a garment made of leather strips and metal rings, all linked together by thin steel wires, all securely fastened tightly around Openshaw's torso, one end attached to his ankles and the other around his neck with a sailor's slipknot in-between. So, every time Openshaw moved his legs, the hawser tightened up; whenever the victim was stimulated, somewhere about his body, goodness knows where, his legs gave an involuntary kick causing strangulation. My assessment was compounded by the state of the skin around his throat, which was inflamed, with a blooming white welt of fat surrounding the wound, still a ghastly bright red (because death had occurred only two minutes before).

'I say, Holmes. There can be no doubt that Openshaw was asphyxiated to death, poor chap, but hold on! There is something else...'

What I noticed made my skin tingle -- the apple in his mouth was not an apple!

'Death by Seville orange!' said Holmes, who had crawled across the carpet from the window looking for footprints and was now standing next to me. 'Am I not correct, Doctor?'

And maybe his speculation was perfectly accurate because there was a large orange protruding from Openshaw's mouth. I crouched down and inspected the affected area more carefully. The cartilage of the temporomandibular joint had been wrenched apart by a sudden and powerful trauma to the maxilla and mandible, widening both of them beyond their full extent. It was impossible to see the incisors, which were sunk deep into the flesh of the fruit. There could be no doubt that orange had been rammed into Openshaw's mouth with tremendous force. Pith and juice were still running down the neck and onto the fine velvet padding of the bench. I used my forefinger to scrape a sample of the juice from the skin and popped it into my mouth. I stood up and looked at Holmes, straight in the eyes.

'No, no, no,' I replied. 'This is a sweet orange, not a bitter one. I would say that it is a Hamlin.'

'But the Seville is a bitter sweet orange.'

'This juice has a flavour that is sweet bitter.'

'Hmmm...' The great detective pondered a while, his right hand now cupping his chin. He extracted a magnifying glass from his pocket and assembled it with dexterity and speed. He leaned in to the corpse and inspected the citrus fruit.

'Ah!' he cried triumphantly. 'Of course, Doctor, is it not obvious? This orange is of irregular shape and form.'

'Aren't they all, Holmes?'

'Some more than others. This fruit is particularly marked, its skin notable for its unusually prominent ridges in random profile.' Then, he too stuck his forefinger into the juice on Openshaw's neck and tasted it. He rolled the liquid around his palate with his tongue and thought more about it.

'THIS is a Guntar sour orange, more commonly known as a Kitchli.'

'Oh well done Holmes! Yes, you are absolutely correct. I recognise the flavour now from my army days. It looks like a Kitchli and it tastes like a Kitchli.'

'*Citrus maderaspatana*. Its country of origin being...'

'India!'

'Absolutely correct, Watson! I believe Pondicherry has spread its influence across the Empire, from far away India to London. Therefore, there can be only one plausible explanation for this murder, for it is murder, my friend, without doubt.'

'Well, Holmes' I queried, 'I wouldn't be so sure. To me this looks like an experiment in a more eclectic area of eroticism where asphyxiation heightens the senses of the brain at the moment of climax, or ecstasy, to a transcendental state that is far in excess of what is experienced in normal sexual activity.'

'No, Watson. The "K.K.K." has struck again, of that there can be absolutely no shadow of a doubt. Regard the window over there. It was wide open. Why, on such a dark and stormy night as this, would these girls have opened it? A person, or persons unknown, have been intruders in this room tonight.'

'Is there any evidence of who they may be, Holmes?'

'The rain has extinguished many of the clues that may have been here, but we are not lost. On the carpet there are traces of two strangers entering this room tonight, but of that there is no surprise. We knew that if Openshaw braved the matter out, death would unfailingly come upon him in some strange and unforeseen manner. So perfect was the organisation of the "K.K.K.," and so systematic its methods, that there is hardly a case upon record where any man succeeded in braving with impunity, or in which any of its outrages were traced home to the perpetrators. In the year 1869, the movement suddenly collapsed.

You will observe that the breaking up of the society was coincident with the disappearance of Openshaw from America with their papers. It may well have been the cause and effect. It is no wonder that he and his family have some of the more implacable spirits upon their track. His register and diary must implicate some of the first men in the South, and many will not sleep at night until it is recovered.'

Holmes was about to reveal more when he was interrupted by a knock on the door. It caught his attention because of its tap-tap-tap style being so different from the furious thump-thump-thump knocking of earlier. I did not mention previously, dear mystery-followers, the constant thumping on the door during our forensic examination. Holmes and I recognised the identity of the tap-tap-tap knocker only too well.

'Ah! Madame! Would you be so kind, Doctor, as to tend to the ladies whilst I unlock the door for her.'

'Ladies? Oh, yes, of course...'

I walked over to the Billericay Beauties, who were standing by the sideboard, their backs facing the room, probably to obscure their sight of Openshaw. The pretty Kayleigh and the fetching Sheneequa were making best efforts to calm their nerves with a bottle of cognac, which was surprising because their reputation for steadfastness was legendary. It was the Right Honourable Benjamin Disraeli, who created the soubriquet of Billericay Beauties on a visit in 1877 as "an intrepid pleasure-seeker who survived the pleasure" and, what with him being our prime minister, his nickname had spread rapidly through London culture, as had the reputation of the girls. I knew, by previous experience, that an appointment with Kayleigh and Sheneequa was a "step into the unknown" for anyone, man or woman, their lure being a far cry from a quality missionary, a dusky duet or the many exotic specialities that the clientele of Mother Kelly's was accustomed to or, indeed, travelled many miles to seek out. Some simply didn't survive the strains of an experience with this duo, their heart being too feeble or their mind too lucid. The girls had seen death on many occasions, so it seemed strange to me that they were so unsettled by Openshaw. I had to find out why.

'Good evening, girls.' I pointed towards Openshaw. 'I believe that that brings your tally of 'kills" to five.'

'Oh, you are a one, Doc!' said Sheneequa, 'it's nearly ten!'

'My God! Nine?'

'Nah. I just told you: it's nearly ten.'

'And what about this chap here?'

'Yeah, we did the sucklin' pig on 'im,' said Kayleigh, 'but we didn't do 'im in.'

'Nah, we didn't do for 'im,' Sheneequa confirmed. 'We set 'im up but we didn't kill 'im. It was two big, hairy blokes came straight through that window! One had tatts all over 'im! Sailors, I reckons...'

'GIRLS!' barked the piercing voice of Mother Kelly in an orotund tone that was impossible to ignore -- if she had been a man, she would have been a legendary regimental sergeant major – 'HERE! NOW!' The girls severed our conversation without hesitation and walked over to her. Then, Madame's green eyes bored into mine.

Mother Kelly ran the finest knocking shop in London Town.

'And Dr. Watson,' she cooed, swiftly modulating to her most compassionate intonation. 'Please, don't leave us all lonely over here.' And then she noticed that Sherlock Holmes was examining the remains of Openshaw.

'You look furtive, Sherlock. Stop it!' Holmes straightened up immediately. Once again, Mother Kelly had changed her tone to suit her requirements. I think that her ability to throw her voice on a whim was a key element to her success.

I joined them just in time to see Mother Kelly hand the girls over to one of the club's footmen, and to hear her passing advice.

'Don't you go fretting now, Kayleigh,' said Madame. 'You *know* that when the club has an *accident* like this, you *know* what we do. It's hardly your first time now, is it girls? I'll give you a safe passage out of town.'

Both of the girls tried to protest their innocence of manslaughter, but Madame quashed their witterings ruthlessly. She stepped forwards sternly and held up her forefinger.

'YOU WILL enjoy a well-earned rest on the Dorset coast. YOU WILL return here in December, in time for the seasonal festivities. Now, away with you!'

The Beauties submitted to silence and were escorted out of the room by the club bullies, the last one pulling the door close. Now, we were alone. Mother Kelly gave us a stern look. I returned the compliment with one of wonder and admiration because, my goodness, she was a sight to behold! She was a good six foot tall with the figure of a Greek goddess – Zeus would have rogered her whilst Hera put the cat out – and a long face of strong, prominent features: a high brow, a nose that was a mixture of the snub and the bulbous, a sensual mouth and then there was the allure of those previously mentioned lustrous green eyes. But these were minor court cards in comparison to her principal asset, which was her sex appeal, where she held a grand slam in spades. Her whole being simply oozed the type of feminine magnetism that men find irresistible. She was also very amusing and witty, with a turn of phrase that only the Irish can muster.

'There! Now that was a party pooper!' said Mother Kelly, smacking her hands together in resolution. I watched the way she did it, momentarily spellbound. Even her simplest of movements held an attraction that caused me a stirring in the trouser department.

'No police, Madame?' I enquired.

'The police?' said she, pointing to Openshaw. 'The police will be picking him out of the eddies down by the Bridge, once he has been cleaned up.' She looked down at the victim's face. 'Now there's a stranger passed happy. Should we tread careful now?'

'This is Mr. John Openshaw, of Horsham. He is a victim of circumstance, of no particular notoriety, an unfortunate pawn in a game of life and death that stretches far beyond these shores, part of a conspiracy to retrieve important papers from his family.'

'Fine,' said Mother Kelly, standing up straight. 'There'll be no fuss.' She looked down at Openshaw and shook her head in dismay. 'The suckling pig does it again.'

Holmes and I shot a glance at one another, which meant that he was entreating me to ask the schoolboy question.

'Madame, what is the suckling pig?'

'This gentleman is wearing what we in the profession call a Devil's Corset. If they move on to the oil and the fruit, it becomes a suckling pig. Who would have thought that, eh?'

'He looks like a Spaniard's Sunday lunch!' I quipped.

'He does that too, Doctor!' and she chuckled, bless her. 'It's a little tasty morsel too far for some, though...' She paused and looked straight at me. 'But you can never question the girls. They like to play the fetish hard, don't they just, but they know that they're a dab hand, eh Doctor?'

Madame was referring to my experience with them a while back. She nudged me, cajoled me, laughing at the same time, her body convulsing against mine. Major stirrings in the trouser department!

'What sort of fetish, Madame?' barked Holmes.

Mother Kelly turned on her seductress voice, whilst laughing and still holding on to me, maybe spurred on by the great detective's apparent naivety. 'Do I have to spell it out to you. Mr. Holmes?'

'Yes, you do,' said he, looking awkward because we were discussing a part of life in which he scored a big, fat zero in my score-chart. 'I need to know all of the details, please.'

Mother Kelly let go of me, composed herself and drew a deep breath. 'The Devil's Corset is an eclectic area of eroticism where asphyxiation heightens the senses of the brain at the moment of climax, or ecstasy, to a transcendental state that is far in excess of what is experienced in normal sexual activity.'

'There!' I ejaculated, triumphantly. 'What did I tell you?!'

I'll swear Holmes blanched for a (very rare) moment before crouching down and applying his exquisite forensic methods to Openshaw's corpse. He spent the next few minutes moving his hands up and down the torso, probing with his long fingers, feeling and prodding, and studying close up with his magnifying glass. Mother Kelly emitted the occasional grunt of approval and, during a particularly deep cleft in the examination, she gave a small gasp.

'My word, Mr. Holmes,' whispered Madame huskily, her eyes transfixed, 'your corporeal knowledge serves you well.' I studied Madame; the rapid breathing; the beads of perspiration on the lip; the slow gyration of her hips. I made my professional diagnosis: she was getting a little warm under the collar!

Holmes ignored her. He took a hold of Openshaw's head and assessed the scope of its axial movement, jigging it up and down and side-to-side. Then, he stood up to his full height. He placed the palm of his right hand on top of the head and delved his two middle fingers into the eye sockets. He gripped the orange with his left hand and tensed up his muscles into a brace position.

'You are absolutely certain, Madame, that the corpse will be cleaned up before disposal?'

Madame nodded. Both of us knew what was coming next and we closed our eyes in anticipation. Without further ado, Holmes wrenched his arms apart with all his might. A CRACK! cut through the charged atmosphere, like a piece of wood snapping in thick mud, and shattered our resolve – both Madame and

I wavered at the sound. When we dared to restore our vision there was Holmes, standing up straight, holding the Kitchli orange up to the light and studying it. What he was analysing was the stalk, two inches still projecting from the top of the fruit where it had been cut from the tree, with what I assumed to be Openshaw's gore dripping off it.

'Ah! See here, Watson!' he cried. 'I was right! When two men – intruders, on a mission – made their way into the room through that window there, they found their prey tied up, already prepared for them. After a moment, when they stood here and reflected upon their good fortune, they went about their grisly business. They forced this orange down his gullet with the strength of a steam hammer. The stalk penetrated the brain of young John Openshaw. He died instantly. That, my dear Doctor, is the end of that!'

Mother Kelly had steadied herself. 'Just who were these two tinkers, Mr. Holmes? And where did they come from?'

'They were members of the "K.K.K." The Ku Klux Klan. A society from America.'

'A society whose members never use the front door,' I quipped, dead straight.

'Ignore him, Madame... The Ku Klux Klan is a society in America that has a ruthless streak of adherence to its rules. We had only been interviewing our client for the first time this evening when we established that his life was in great danger from this "K.K.K." We accompanied him on his way to Waterloo Station.'

'Well, well, well Mr. Holmes,' said Madame, 'we both lost a paying client this evening. Let's chalk this one up on the board and raise a glass to future fortunes!'

Holmes nodded. He walked over to the sideboard and placed the orange on top. He withdrew a penknife and applied its blade to the skin, ripping open the fruit and removing some of the pips. He tucked them into a handkerchief, folded the blade back into its case and placed the whole package into his pocket. He turned to face us, and what a sight he was! His clothing in disarray, his hair dishevelled but with three balloons of cognac in his hands, which were still covered in blood and brains. He handed one to each of us and raised his to the heavens.

'Madame! I salute you! You bear the most resolute constitution. You run the finest establishment in London. And...'

'... and I am still the finest tumble in town! *Leanna!*' Death to the murderers of our clients!

We downed our brandies in one cheerful gulp.

* * *

The weather had cleared in the morning and the sun was shining with a subdued brightness through the dim veil which hangs over this great city. Sherlock Holmes was already at breakfast when I came into the drawing room.

'You will excuse me for not waiting for you,' said he; 'I have, I foresee, a very busy day before me, in looking into this case of young Openshaw's.'

'Is it not a little too late for that, Holmes? What steps will you take?'

'I shall find the perpetrators of this murder, Watson. No matter what I do next.'

'But, my friend, who will pay us when the client is deceased?'

'Money? What is the value of money when the taking of an innocent life occurs under our very noses?'

'Holmes, you may like to try that line of reasoning with Mrs. Hudson when she ambushes me every five minutes about the overdue rent. I doubt that she will indulge you.'

'Tsk! We have no means at all?'

'None. Last night's cab driver took my last guinea. Just of late, we have worked for non-paying clients. We are as poor as church mice, but our landlady is heartless and demands payment.'

'Oh, piffle to Mrs. Hudson! You must negotiate with her. In the meantime, I shall head over to the City to commence my investigation.'

'I shall find some breakfast first.'

'Just ring the bell and our landlady's maid will bring your first beverage of the day.'

It was one tug of the cord for coffee; two for Earl Grey; and three for Lapsang Souchong. As I waited, I lifted the unopened newspaper from the table and glanced my eye over it. It rested upon a headline, which was no surprise to me.

'I say, Holmes, look at this...' I said, as my eye has caught this headline: '"Tragedy Near Waterloo Bridge."'

'Ah!' he said, laying down his cup. 'Mother Kelly's boys moved swiftly. Pray, read it out loud Watson.'

'It says here: "Police Constable Cook, of H Division, on duty near Waterloo Bridge, heard a cry for help and a splash in the water. The night, however, was extremely dark and stormy, so that, in spite of the help of several passersby, it was quite impossible to affect a rescue. The alarm, however, was given, and, by the aid of the water police, the body was eventually recovered. It proved to be that of a young gentleman whose name, as it appears from an envelope which was found in his pocket, was John Openshaw, and whose residence is near Horsham. It is conjectured that he may have been hurrying down to catch the last train from Waterloo Station, and that in his haste and the extreme darkness, he missed the path and walked over the edge of one of the small landing-places for river steamboats. The body exhibited traces of violence around the jaw, which indicates a heavy fall took place, and there can be no doubt that the deceased had been the victim of an unfortunate accident."'

'There you go,' said Holmes. 'The bungling Police at Scotland Yard will believe anything they care to dream up for themselves.'

We sat in silence for some minutes, Holmes more depressed than usual by the turn-out of events in any of our cases together.

'This mystery – this case – hurts my pride, Watson,' he said at last. 'It is a petty feeling, no doubt, but it hurts my pride. It becomes a personal matter with me now, and, if God sends me health, I shall set my hand upon this gang. That Openshaw should come to me for help, and that I should be sitting a few feet away from him when he met his death!'

All of a sudden, he sprang from his chair and paced about the room in uncontrollable agitation, with a flush upon his sallow cheeks, and a nervous clasping and unclasping of his long, thin hands.

'They must be cunning devils!' he exclaimed at last. 'How could they have climbed up two floors of the Kingly Street knocking-shop in those terrible conditions and without me knowing?'

'They are sailors!' mollified I. 'Climbing is in their blood, all that rope and rigging, what? I think that maybe they had a long ladder and they employed an accomplice to stand on the ground outside and steady it for them in those high winds?'

'Well, Watson, I think that you are correct. They are resourceful. But so am I. We shall see who will win in the long run.'

I could hear the maid's footsteps on the landing, on a mission to deliver my three-tug Lapsang Souchong. Holmes cocked an ear, then moved as fast as a cat over to the coat stand, scooped up his hat and coat and cane, and opened the door for the maid.

'I am going out now,' he said. 'Good day to you, Mrs. Hudson!'

Ambushed! I was about to pay interest on the rent arrears.

* * *

All day long I was engaged in my professional work, and it was late in the evening before I returned to Baker Street. Sherlock Holmes had not come back yet. It was nearly ten o'clock before he entered, looking pale and worn. He walked up to the sideboard, and tearing a piece from the loaf, he devoured it voraciously, washing it down with a long draught of water.

'You are hungry,' I remarked.

'Starving. It had escaped my memory. I have had nothing since breakfast.'

'Nothing?'

'Not a bite. I had not time to think of it.'

'And how have you succeeded?'

'Well.'

'You have a clue?'

'I have them in the hollow of my hand. Young Openshaw shall not remain long unavenged. Why, Watson, let us put their own devilish trademark upon them. It is well thought of!'

'What do you mean?'

He took his handkerchief from his trouser pocket. He tipped out the pips upon the table that he had foraged the night before. Of these he took five and thrust them into an envelope. On the inside of the flap he wrote, "S.H. for J.C." Then he sealed it and addressed it to "Captain James Calhoun, Barque *Lone Star*, Savannah, Georgia."

'That will await him when he enters port,' said he, chuckling. 'It may give him a sleepless night. He will find it as a sure precursor of his fate as Openshaw did before him.'

'And who is this Captain Calhoun?'

'The leader of the "K.K.K." gang. I shall have the others, but he first.'

'How did you trace it, then?'

He took a large sheet of paper from his pocket, all covered with dates and names.

'I have spent the whole day,' said he, 'looking over Lloyd's registers and the files of old papers, following the future career of every vessel which touched at Pondicherry in January and February in '83. There were thirty-six ships of fair tonnage which were reported there during these months. Of these, the *Lone Star* instantly attracted my attention, since, although it was reported as having cleared from London, the name is that which is given to one of the states of the Union.'

'Texas, I think.'

'I was not and am not sure which; but I knew that the ship must have an American origin.'

What then?'

'I searched the Dundee records, and when I found that the barque *Lone Star* was there in January, '85, my suspicions became a certainty. I then inquired as to vessels which lay at present in the port of London.'

'Yes?'

'The *Lone Star* arrived there last week. I went down to the Albert Dock and found that she had been taken down the river by the early tide this morning, homeward bound to Savannah. I wired to Gravesend and learned that she had passed some time ago, and as the wind is easterly, I have no doubt that she is now past the Goodwins, and not very far from the Isle of Wight.'

'So, Holmes, Goodwin Sands is in Essex. The Isle of Wight, which usually sits just south of the counties of West Sussex and Hampshire has now, miraculously, overnight, shifted itself one hundred miles east to Kent?'

'Nobody likes a smart-Alec, Watson.'

'Apart from the smart-Alec himself, who, in my score chart of your abilities, gave you only two points for geography, remember? Anyway, what will you do next?'

'Oh, I have my hand upon Captain Calhoun. He and the two mates are, as I learn, the only native-born Americans on the ship. The others are Finns and Germans. I also know that there were three away from the ship last night. I had it from the stevedore, who has been loading their cargo. By the time their sailing ship reaches Savannah the mailboat will have carried this letter, and the cable will have informed the police of Savannah that these three gentlemen are badly wanted here upon a charge of murder.'

'SENSATIONAL!' I cried, standing up and applauding his incisive research and brilliant actions. 'Let's go out and celebrate and find you some supper, before you expire from hunger.'

Two minutes later we were heading down the staircase at a pace when the doorbell rang. We skidded to a halt on the treads, crouched down and waited. Sure enough, Mrs. Hudson emerged from her apartment.

'Don't move a muscle,' I mouthed at Holmes, and gesticulated in sign language that she was relentless on the warpath for the rent.

There was a brief conversation on the doorstep and then she welcomed in two gentlemen dressed in black frock coats and dull top hats.

'Undertakers,' I said.

'For poor Nanny...'

'Now, if we move quickly,' I whispered, 'we can escape before they bring her out. Show a leg, Holmes!'

I hastened ahead downstairs with stealth, making as little noise as possible. The great detective was hot on my heels. We reached the front door unseen and I ran pell-mell outside, and straight into a very tall gentleman, dressed exquisitely in evening tie adorned with a cape and sporting a shiny silk top hat. It was a violent collision, but he caught me, and I was now in his embrace. I was looking into a face best-described as that of a pugilist's guardian angel – a tough and resolute visage with the distinguished features of an aristocrat but the flattened nose and square jaw of a boxer, and a well-tonsured facial hair arrangement of moustache and bugger-bars adorning the whole. At the moment of impact that face bore an expression of languid composure, as if the gentleman was previously employed to be my saviour. However, within a split second, he metamorphosised into a rabid dog! His cheeks lifted. His lips curled back to bare his teeth. His jaw dropped. His eyes sprang open, all red and veiny and pulsating! He bellowed at me like an angry lion, roaring with all his might! Suddenly, he lifted me up, and threw me aside across the pavement with such immense power that I ended up sideways in the street gutter.

Holmes had stopped short and stood back a yard or two from our newly-acquainted ogre.

'Bad night out, Teddy?'

'Don't you dare call me Teddy!' rasped he.

'Here to collect Nanny?'

'DON'T YOU DARE CALL HER NANNY!' he cried out loud.

'Most things in my life are a dare, Moriarty.'

MORIARTY! The master criminal that never dirtied his hands. The killer that never killed his victims. The murderer who never murdered anyone. The lingering menace in Sherlock Holmes's life since childhood, or thereabouts...

'She chose to spend her last moments on this Earth with me.' Holmes paused a moment for devilish dramatic effect. 'Instead of you.'

Oh, he just had to rub it in to this angry monster, didn't he? And, sure enough, he received the reaction he desired. Professor Moriarty became enraged, snarling and pacing furiously, on the point of pouncing at Holmes. But just as he was about to lunge, the two undertakers emerged from the house carrying a stretcher between them bearing the body of Nanny Moriarty. Mrs. Hudson followed them out; when she noticed me climbing out of the Baker Street sluices, she ran over to help me, her extraneous reaction to my predicament betraying her true feelings. This did not go unnoticed by Holmes and Moriarty.

'Sherlock? I presume *that* is Dr. Watson?'

'Yes, Teddy' said Holmes nonchalantly. 'It is thanks to Dr. Watson that your mother's final hour was peaceful. Watson officiated and made full use of his medicines. There was no pain or anxiety.'

Moriarty strode over to me. He offered me his hand and I took it. Words cannot describe the look in his eyes; of pain and relief, and gratitude. Then, he dropped a small velvet sack into my hand that "chinked" on landing.

'Doctor, I am most grateful my mother did not suffer.' Then, he produced his calling card and handed it to me. 'And I apologise to you profusely for not curbing my temper. Please send me your tailor's account for the cleaning and repairs to your suit.'

He made a bow, turned on his heel and strode towards his carriage, which was located behind the

On first impression, I thought that Professor Moriarty came across as a thoroughly decent chap!

undertakers' funeral cart. He was a man of bearing and elegance, and he was a good mover. He glanced at Holmes, and I am sure that I heard him issue a threat along the lines of: "I am on your case..." but I could have been wrong, before he stepped up and closed the door. The great detective watched him without a response or, indeed, any recognition. With a gentle ripple of the undertakers' reins, the cortege of two slipped off down Baker Street.

And that, dear reader, was my first encounter with Professor "Teddy" Moriarty. It was not the last – there were terrible moments to come that I was blissfully unaware of. It was, however, the last I saw of the small velvet sack, which was whisked away by Mrs. Hudson to cover our overdue rent. I never found out how much gold it contained, but there was no cause for an ambush of intimacy by our landlady for the rest of that year. Well, apart from Christmas Day.

As for the murderers of John Openshaw, even the best laid of human plans may go asunder. Captain Calhoun and his accomplices were never to receive the orange pips which would show them that another man, as cunning and as resolute as themselves, was upon their track. Very long and severe were the equinoctial gales that year. We waited long for news of the *Lone Star* of Savannah, but none ever reached us. We did at last hear that somewhere far out in the Atlantic a shattered sternpost of a boat was seen swinging in the trough of a wave, with the letters "L.S." carved upon it, and that is all which we shall ever know of the fate of the *Lone Star*.